This Box  belongs to

. . . .

www.boxerbooks.com

To my Lily, Skyla and Sonny for their love and inspiration,
to Jodie for her support and loveliness and to
David and Leilani for their wonderful energy and enthusiasm.

First published in Great Britain in hardback in 2015
First published in Great Britain in paperback in 2016
by Boxer® Books Limited.
www.boxerbooks.com
Boxer® is a registered trademark of Boxer Books Limited.

The illustrations were screen printed by the author.
The text is set in Goudy Old Style.

ISBN 978-1-910126-75-2

1 3 5 7 9 10 8 6 4 2

Printed in China

Lily and Bear

Lisa Stubbs

Boxer Books

Lily loved to draw.
She drew
cats and girls,
birds and boats,
and houses
and hearts.

She drew the sea
and a pirate ship
and a teapot.

She drew tricycles
and a banjo.

And then she drew . . .

Bear.

Lily loved Bear and Bear loved Lily.

Lily took Bear by the paw . . .

They attended royal tea parties

and sailed carpet seas.

They did Lily's favourite thing
and drew BIG pictures.

Then they raced
around on tricycles.

But best of all,
they sang really
loudly while
Bear played
the banjo
brilliantly.

Lily loved Bear and Bear loved Lily.

After a while, Bear sat down.

He didn't want to attend royal tea parties, sail pirate ships or ride tricycles any more. Bear wanted to do Bear things.

Lily loved Bear and Bear loved Lily so Bear took Lily by the hand . . .

They picked
huckleberries,
and ate them
from Bear's paws.

They caught
slippery jumping
fish in the river.

They did Bear's favourite thing and scratched their backs on a knotty pine.

Then
they rolled
down the
mountainside.

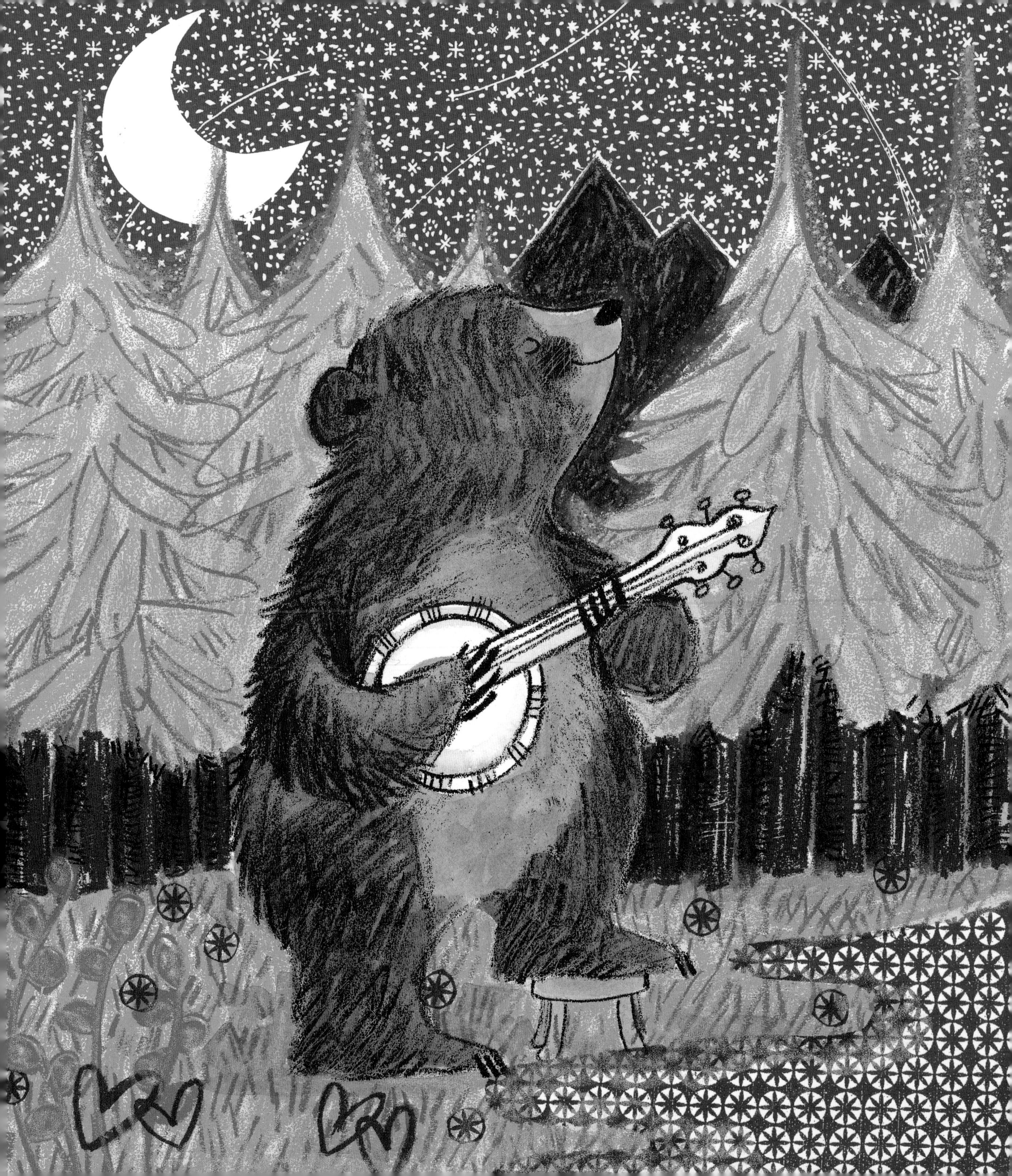

But best of all, as the stars
started to shine, they sang
a really quiet song while
Bear gently played the banjo
brilliantly until . . .

. . . it was time to
sleep and dream of
their next adventure.

"I love you, Bear."
"And I love you, Lily."

More Boxer Books paperbacks to enjoy

Clip-Clop
by Nicola Smee
Voted one of the top 50 picture books in the past 25 years – Huffington Post.

Cat, Dog, Pig and Duck all want to climb aboard Mr Horse for a ride. But when they get bored with the slow pace, they ask Mr Horse to go faster and faster ... But will "faster" lead to disaster? A delightful rhythmical text with adorable illustrations that will enthral every child.

How Rocket Learnt to Read
by Tad Hills

Rocket is an irresistible puppy who is not the least bit interested in reading – he'd much prefer to be chasing leaves, chewing sticks or listening to the birds sing. But one day, while trying to take a nap, Rocket unexpectedly finds himself in the classroom of a very determined little bird who captures his imagination with her lively stories. Together, they learn to read, one glorious letter at a time!